§ ═══ SADDLEBACK *Classics* ═══ §

STUDY GUIDE

Macbeth

WILLIAM SHAKESPEARE

Date: 1/9/12

SADDLEBACK
EDUCATIONAL PUBLISHING

SADDLEBACK *Classics*

Hamlet

Julius Caesar

Macbeth

The Merchant of Venice

A Midsummer Night's Dream

Othello

Romeo and Juliet

The Tempest

Development and Production: Laurel Associates, Inc.
Cover Art: Black Eagle Productions

SADDLEBACK
EDUCATIONAL PUBLISHING

Website: www.sdlback.com

ISBN-13: 978-1-56254-611-3
ISBN-10: 1-56254-611-2
eBook: 978-1-60291-409-4

Printed in the United States of America
15 14 13 12 11 5 6 7 8 9

CONTENTS

THE PROGRAM

Saddleback Classics were expressly designed to help students with limited reading ability gain access to some of the world's greatest literature. While retaining the essence and stylistic "flavor" of the original, each *Saddleback Classic* has been expertly adapted to a reading level that never exceeds grade 4.0.

An ideal introduction to later, more in-depth investigations of the original works, *Saddleback Classics* utilize a number of strategies to ensure the involvement of reluctant readers: airy, uncomplicated page design, shortened sentences, easy-reading type style, elimination of archaic words and spellings, shortened total book length, and handsome illustrations.

THE STUDY GUIDES

The *Saddleback Classics Study Guides* provide a wealth of reproducible support materials to help students extend the learning experience. Features include critical background notes on both the author and the times, character descriptions, chapter summaries, and seven "universal" exercises which may be used to follow up the reading of any *Saddleback Classics* novel or play.

In addition to the universal exercises, 27 title-specific exercises are included to review, test, and enrich students' comprehension as well as their grasp of important vocabulary and concepts. All reproducible, the worksheets provided for Shakespeare's plays are designed to be used act-by-act as the student's reading of the play proceeds. Several exercises are provided for each act. One always focuses on key vocabulary. Others include a simple comprehension check and treatment of an important literary concept such as character analysis, point of view, inference, or figurative language. A three-page final exam is also included in every *Saddleback Classics Study Guide*.

USING THE STUDY GUIDES

Before assigning any of the reproducible exercises, be sure each student has a personal copy of the *Glossary* and the *Facts About the Author* and *About the Times*. Students will need to be familiar with many of the literary terms in order to complete the worksheets. Obviously, the *Facts About the Author* and *About the Times* lend themselves to any number of writing, art, or research projects you may wish to assign.

The title-specific exercises may be used as a springboard for class discussions or role-playing. Alternatively, you may wish to assign some exercises as homework and others as seatwork during the closing minutes of a class period.

All exercises in this Guide are designed to accommodate independent study as well as group work. The occasional assignment of study partners or competitive teams often enhances interest and promotes creativity.

FACTS ABOUT THE AUTHOR

WILLIAM SHAKESPEARE
(1564–1616)

William Shakespeare is widely regarded as the finest poet and playwright who ever lived. Yet he was the son of illiterate parents and never attended college!

Much of this remarkable man's life is shrouded in mystery. He had been dead almost a hundred years before anyone wrote a short account of his life. But we do know that his mother, Mary Arden, was the daughter of a prosperous farmer. His father, John Shakespeare, was a successful glovemaker who also traded in wool, hides, and grain. They lived in an English market town called Stratford-on-Avon, where William was born in 1564. Their house still stands.

Until the age of 13 or 14, Shakespeare probably attended the Stratford grammar school where he read the great Latin classics of Cicero, Virgil, and Seneca. Some stories say that he had to leave school early because of his father's financial difficulties. But there is no official record of his life until 1582, when he married Anne Hathaway at the age of 18. By 1585, he and Anne had three children. No one knows for sure what happened to him during the next seven years, although one account says that he was a schoolmaster. In 1592, however, records reveal that he was working in London as both an actor and a playwright. By that year, he had published two popular poems and written at least three plays.

Records from various sources show that Shakespeare became wealthy. In 1597, he bought one of the grandest houses in Stratford. (It had 10 fireplaces!) The next year he bought 10 percent of the stock in the handsome Globe Theater and a fine house in London. His artistic life was very busy and productive. His theatrical company, known as the King's Men, presented a variety of plays, week after week. It is thought that he rehearsed in the mornings, acted in the afternoons, and wrote at night.

After 1612, he spent most of his time in Stratford with his family. He died there, at the age of 52, on April 23, 1616. The tomb of the great literary genius still stands at Holy Trinity Church in Stratford.

FACTS ABOUT THE TIMES

In 1564, when Shakespeare was born . . .

About 100,000 people lived in London; the horsedrawn coach was introduced in England; the great Italian sculptor and painter, Michelangelo, died; an outbreak of plague killed more than 20,000 Londoners.

In 1616, when Shakespeare died . . .

Sir Walter Raleigh began his search for El Dorado; tobacco was becoming a popular crop in Virginia; Pocahontas died; the Catholic church forbade Galileo from conducting any further scientific investigations.

FACTS ABOUT THE CHARACTERS

Duncan is the King of Scotland, a good and honorable man who is murdered by Macbeth.

Macbeth is the Scottish Thane (nobleman) of Glamis and a general in Duncan's army.

Lady Macbeth is Macbeth's wife.

Banquo is a thane and a general in Duncan's army. A friend of Macbeth's, he is later murdered by him.

Fleance is Banquo's son. He escapes when his father is murdered.

Malcolm is Duncan's eldest son and heir.

Donalbain is another son of Duncan's.

Macduff is a thane, loyal to Duncan.

Lady Macduff is Macduff's wife. To punish Macduff, Macbeth has her and her family murdered.

Ross is Macduff's cousin.

Lennox is a thane, loyal to Duncan.

Seyton is Macbeth's aide.

Siward is an English earl. He helps Malcolm in the fight against Macbeth.

Young Siward is Siward's son. He bravely faces Macbeth in a duel and is killed.

The Three Witches are supernatural beings who tell Macbeth and Banquo about certain events that will occur in the future.

SUMMARIES BY ACT

ACT 1

Scotland is at war. Near a battlefield, three witches meet during a storm. They plan to greet Macbeth, one of the Scottish generals, before the setting of the sun. Meanwhile, a soldier comes to King Duncan with a report about the battle. He speaks of Macbeth's great bravery on the field. To reward Macbeth for this, Duncan gives him the title *Thane of Cawdor*. That evening, the three witches use this title when they greet Macbeth. They surprise him by predicting that he will soon be king.

They also tell Banquo, another general, that he will be the father of many kings. Later, King Duncan, his sons Malcolm and Donalbain, along with Banquo and other lords, go to Inverness, Macbeth's castle, for a visit. In her wish to be queen, Lady Macbeth encourages her husband to kill Duncan.

ACT 2

While Duncan is sleeping, Macbeth kills him. Lady Macbeth smears the drugged and sleeping guards with Duncan's blood. Early in the morning,

Macduff and Lennox arrive at Inverness, wishing to see Duncan. They discover the body, so Macbeth kills the guards, blaming Duncan's death on them. Duncan's sons flee—Malcolm to England and Donalbain to Ireland. Ross and Macduff assume that Duncan's sons had paid the guards to kill their father. Because the two sons left the country, they appear to be guilty. Macbeth is crowned King of Scotland.

ACT 3

As Banquo thinks about what the witches had said, he realizes that all their words about Macbeth have come true. He remembers the witches' words about his own sons and has strong hopes for their futures. Macbeth arranges with murderers to have Banquo and Fleance killed. As Banquo is being murdered, Fleance escapes. That evening, Macbeth and Lady Macbeth, the new king and queen, welcome guests to a banquet. As guests are seated, Macbeth sees a vision of Banquo's ghost. He speaks to it in such a way that his part in Banquo's death becomes clear. Lady Macbeth orders the guests to leave, saying that her husband is not feeling well. Suspicious of Macbeth, Macduff goes to England. He plans to get King Edward's help in the fight against Macbeth.

ACT 4

Macbeth visits the three witches and asks them about his future. They show him a series of visions that tell the future in the form of riddles. Then the witches disappear, and Lennox arrives.

He reports to Macbeth that Macduff has fled to England. Angry about this news, Macbeth orders the murder of Macduff's wife, children, and any servants who happen to be with them. Murderers arrive at Fife, Macduff's castle, and kill everyone inside. In England, Malcolm and Macduff make plans to restore peace to Scotland. They talk about the help that England's King Edward has promised them. Ross then arrives with news about the murder of Macduff's family. This makes the shocked Macduff even more determined to overthrow Macbeth.

ACT 5

Lady Macbeth appears to have lost her mind. Her doctor says he can do nothing for her. Near Dunsinane, the forces led by Malcolm and Macduff prepare to attack. Malcolm tells his men to hide behind the camouflage of branches cut from the trees of Birnam Wood. As he gets ready for the attack, Macbeth receives the news that Lady Macbeth is dead. He also hears that Birnam Wood is moving toward Dunsinane. He remembers the witches' prophecy: *"Macbeth shall never be beaten until / Birnam Wood comes to Dunsinane Hill,"* and he becomes fearful. Then he also remembers their other prophecy: *"None of woman born shall harm Macbeth,"* so he feels safe again. Later, he finds out that Macduff was not born in the normal way. In a duel, Macduff kills Macbeth. Later, Malcolm becomes King of Scotland.

aside lines spoken by an actor that the other characters on stage supposedly cannot hear; an aside usually shares the character's inner thoughts with the audience

> **Although she appeared to be calm, the heroine's aside revealed her inner terror.**

backstage the part of the theater where actors prepare to go onstage, where scenery is kept, etc.

> **Before entering, the villain impatiently waited backstage.**

cast the entire company of actors performing in a play

> **The entire cast must attend tonight's dress rehearsal.**

character a fictional person or creature in a story or play

> **Mighty Mouse is one of my favorite cartoon characters.**

climax the outcome of the main conflict of a play or novel

> **The outlaw's capture made an exciting climax to the story.**

comedy a funny play, film, or TV show that has a happy ending

> **My friends and I always enjoy a Jim Carrey comedy.**

conflict the struggle between characters, forces, or ideas at the center of a story

> **Dr. Jekyll and Mr. Hyde illustrates the conflict between good and evil.**

dialogue words spoken by the characters in a novel or play

> **Amusing dialogue is an important element of most comedies.**

drama a story, usually not a comedy, especially written to be performed by actors in a play or movie

> **The TV drama about spies was very suspenseful.**

event something that happens; a specific occurrence

> **The most exciting event in the story was the surprise ending.**

figurative language colorful wording not meant to be taken literally, but to form a colorful, sharp picture in the mind

> **A "screaming" headline may be set in large type, but it makes no sound at all.**

introduction a short reading that presents and explains a novel or play

> **The introduction to *Frankenstein* is in the form of a letter.**

motive the internal or external force that makes a character do something

> **What was that character's motive for telling a lie?**

passage a section of a written work, ranging from one line to several paragraphs

> **His favorite passage from the book described the fisherman's childhood.**

playwright the author of a play

> **William Shakespeare is the world's most famous playwright.**

plot the chain of events in a story or play that leads to its final outcome

> **The plot of that mystery story is filled with action.**

point of view the mental position from which a character sees the events of the story unfold

> **The father's point of view about elopement was quite different from the daughter's.**

prologue an introduction to a play that comes before the first act

> **The playwright described the main characters in the prologue to the play.**

quotation a passage quoted; the exact words spoken by a character; the words set off by quotation marks

> **A popular quotation from *Julius Caesar* begins, "Friends, Romans, countrymen, . . ."**

role the part that an actor performs in a play

> **Who would you like to see play the role of Romeo?**

sequence the time-order in which story events take place

> **Sometimes actors rehearse their scenes out of sequence.**

setting where and when the story events take place

> **This play's setting is New York in the 1940s.**

soliloquy a speech in a play in which a character tells his or her thoughts to the audience, as if talking to himself or herself

> **One famous soliloquy is Hamlet's speech that begins, "To be, or not to be . . ."**

symbol a person or thing that stands for, or represents, something else

> **In Hawthorne's famous novel, the scarlet letter is a symbol for adultery.**

theme the central meaning of a play or novel; the main idea

> **Ambition and revenge are common themes in Shakespeare's plays.**

tragedy a serious play with a sad ending

> ***Macbeth*, the shortest of Shakespeare's plays, is a tragedy.**

MACBETH
ANSWER KEY

1 PRE-READING: INTRODUCTION
1. (in 2003) 963; 13–14   2. kills, fearing, killed, oppose, tormented, guilt, suicide   3. one of the witches   4. He looks troubled; he is wearing a Scottish tartan. He looks determined.   5.–6. Answers will vary.   7. No, human nature hasn't changed.

2 COMPREHENSION CHECK: ACT 1
1. a   2. b   3. b   4. a   5. b   6. c   7. c

3 WORDS AND MEANINGS: ACT 1
A.
```
        Y H T L I F
    V A N I S H E D R
    P S T R E N G T H E
    R M   H         P Y
    O U N   U       S T
    P R   I   N     O L
    H D     A   D   R E
    E E       L   P U
    C R         L R   R
    Y F A N T A S I E S C
        S R E G G A D V
        E M B R A C E
```
B. 1. murder   2. filthy   3. thunder   4. villain, vanished   5. fantasies   6. prophecy, prosper   7. Cruelty   8. daggers   9. strength, embrace

4 CHARACTER STUDY: ACT 1
A. Macbeth, soldier, King Duncan, Lady Macbeth, witch, Banquo, Ross
1. soldier   2. Ross   3. Banquo   4. King Duncan   5. witch   6. Lady Macbeth   7. Macbeth
B. 1. Lady Macbeth   2. King Duncan   3. witch   4. Macbeth   5. soldier   6. Ross   7. Banquo

5 SYNONYMS AND ANTONYMS: ACT 1
A. **Across:** 2. weary   3. dismay   5. former   7. truth
Down: 1. treason   3. deeds   4. predict   5. flags   6. heath
B. 1. release   2. hello   3. weakness   4. fresh   5. ordinary   6. failure   7. shallow   8. dull   9. guilty   10. past

6 RECALLING DETAILS: ACT 1
A. 1. T   2. F   3. T   4. F   5. T
B. 1. Macbeth and Banquo meet **three** witches on a heath near Forres.   2. The witches tell Macbeth that **he** will be king - or - The witches tell **Banquo** that **he** will be king.   3. Banquo completely **does not trust** what the witches have said.   4. Duncan appoints his **oldest** son **Malcolm** as his successor.
C. 1. in a letter   2. Duncan must be killed   3. located in a pleasant place   4. guards

7 COMPREHENSION CHECK: ACT 2
1. b   2. b   3. c   4. c   5. a   6. b   7. a

8 WORDS AND MEANINGS: ACT 2
A.
```
    L     L L E W E R A F
  S O   S U O I R E S
  L   C Y       C
  U A   A   F D   R R
  M R   L R R     E E
  B R   I       A B
  E I   E G     M M
  R E   W H E     A
  I   D   T   N H
  N     L I K E L Y O C
  G       N       D
  S E C R E T
```
B. 1. frighten, scream   2. farewell   3. likely, done   4. weird   5. loyal   6. chamber, slumbering   7. serious   8. carried, secret

9 CHARACTER STUDY: ACT 2
A. Banquo, Macduff, Macbeth, Lady Macbeth, Lennox, Malcolm, Ross, Donalbain
1. Macbeth   2. Banquo   3. Malcolm   4. Donalbain   5. Lady Macbeth   6. Macduff and Lennox   7. Ross
B. 1. Lady Macbeth   2. Donalbain   3. Ross   4. Lennox   5. Malcolm   6. Macduff   7. Banquo   8. Macbeth

10 SYNONYMS AND ANTONYMS: ACT 2
A. **Across:** 1. fatal   3. mock   4. mood   6. separated   7. wicked
Down: 1. foolish   2. mad   4. motive   5. wailing
B. 1. wastefulness   2. artificial   3. first   4. restores   5. dirty   6. waking   7. arriving   8. rough   9. kind   10. good

11 ANALYZING SIMILES AND METAPHORS: ACT 2
2. simile   3. metaphor   4. metaphor   5. metaphor   6. metaphor
Examples will vary.

12 COMPREHENSION CHECK: ACT 3
1. b   2. c   3. a   4. b   5. c   6. a   7. b

13 WORDS AND MEANINGS: ACT 3
A.
```
          G R A C I O U S
    F
  G O S       S T B U O D
  N R D   S     N
  I T O   T T N E M L I A
  S U H   S   D
  S N T   E   H I     H
  E E E   U   E C   T S
  L M   G   A C U K
  B       L A O   S
  B A N Q U E T Y   A
        H   M
```
B. 1. blessing, health   2. masks   3. guests, banquet   4. doubts   5. gracious   6. youth, accident   7. methods, fortune   8. ailment

14 CHARACTER STUDY: ACT 3
A. 1. Lord   2. Banquo   3. Murderer 1 and Murderer 2   4. Macbeth   5. Lennox   6. Lady Macbeth

B. 1. Banquo 2. Lord 3. Lady Macbeth
4. Macbeth 5. Lennox 6. Murderer 2
7. Murderer 1

15 SYNONYMS AND ANTONYMS: ACT 3
A. **ACROSS:** 2. country 4. champion
6. reckless 8. wish 9. proper
DOWN: 1. dreadful 3. enrage
5. drowse 7. shape
B. 1. weak 2. guilty 3. lively 4. sorrowful
5. proud 6. sickness 7. better
8. expose 9. admit 10. honor

16 FINDING CAUSE AND EFFECT: ACT 3
2. The murderers agree to kill Banquo and
Fleance. 3. Fleance is able to escape.
4. The murderer comes to the banquet to
report to Macbeth. 5. Lady Macbeth is
concerned that Macbeth is not being gracious
to the guests. 6. Macbeth is startled.
7. Macbeth acts strangely. 8. Macbeth
continues to act strangely. 9. Macbeth
decides to send a spy to Macduff's castle.
10. Lennox goes to England to help Malcolm.

17 COMPREHENSION CHECK: ACT 4
1. a 2. c 3. c 4. b 5. a 6. c 7. a

18 WORDS AND MEANINGS: ACT 4
A.
```
T R U S T W O R T H Y
F Y       R   N C
O G     E   V A O
R N     F I   T M
E I   F   R L   U M
S T U   T U     R A
T S   U F P     A N
    O R   E   R L D
    U E     E     O
S W     W     W   M
  O S W A M P     U
    P       Q U A R R E L S
```
B. 1. virtuous 2. natural, weep
3. Quarrels 4. suffer, trustworthy
5. command 6. swamp, forest
7. rumor 8. powerful, stingy

19 CHARACTER STUDY: ACT 4
A. 1. Ross 2. Malcolm 3. Vision 2
4. Witches 5. Lady Macduff
6. Macbeth 7. Macduff
B. 1. Malcolm 2. Witches 3. Macduff
4. Ross 5. Lady Macduff 6. Macbeth
7. Vision 2

20 SYNONYMS AND ANTONYMS: ACT 4
A. **ACROSS:** 1. faults 4. cauldron
6. traitor 7. throbs 9. permission
DOWN: 2. appease 3. enemies
5. greedy 8. harm
B. 1. weak 2. doubtful 3. appear
4. fortunate 5. deceptive 6. gentle
7. poverty 8. noisy 9. public
10. virtues

21 ANALOGIES: ACT 4
1. work 2. rain 3. calm 4. loyalty
5. ask 6. wool

22 COMPREHENSION CHECK: ACT 5
1. b 2. a 3. c 4. a 5. c 6. a 7. b

23 WORDS AND MEANINGS: ACT 5
A.
```
      D E L I X E   P
  M E D I C I N E   E
S         S W   R
T   E     S   O F Y
R   G I E F U R Y U H
U   N     T   M T
T   T V E   H E L
S   I   I   L   S A
W   T   L     E
      E T Y R A N T H
M O U R N I N G   H
              C
```
B. 1. witness 2. tyrant 3. medicine,
healthy 4. mourning 5. struts
6. fury 7. perfumes, worth
8. challenge, invite 9. exiled

24 CHARACTER STUDY: ACT 5
A. 1. Doctor 2. Ross 3. Malcolm
4. Lady Macbeth 5. Macbeth
6. Gentlewoman 7. Seyton
B. 1. Gentlewoman 2. Lady Macbeth
3. Seyton 4. Macbeth 5. Ross
6. Malcolm 7. Doctor

25 SYNONYMS AND ANTONYMS: ACT 5
A. **ACROSS:** 1. command 4. yield
6. divine 7. strength 8. wretched
DOWN: 1. cure 2. disease 3. visions
5. taunted
B. 1. never 2. forgiveness 3. destroying
4. remembered 5. important 6. genius
7. cowardly 8. quietly 9. defeat
10. friends

26 CONSIDERING POINT OF VIEW: ACT 5
1. Malcolm 2. Gentlewoman 3. Lady Macbeth
4. Macbeth 5. Malcolm 6. Gentlewoman
7. Doctor 8. Macduff 9. Lady Macbeth
10. Macduff 11. Doctor 12. Macbeth

27 LOOKING BACK
Answers will vary.

28 FINAL EXAM: Part 1
1. c 2. a 3. d 4. a 5. b 6. d

FINAL EXAM: Part 2
(Answers should be in complete sentences.)
1. . . . so they won't be able to deny
committing the murder. 2. . . . because she
feels guilty. 3. . . . because he doesn't
want the witches' prophecy to come true.
4. . . . because he wants to help Malcolm,
and he never imagined Macbeth would kill
his family. 5. . . . because she is suffering
so much. 6. They made Macbeth think he
was invulnerable when, of course, he wasn't.

FINAL EXAM: Part 3
1. 8, escapes 2. 9, banquet
3. 3, visits 4. 1, courage 5. 13, walks
6. 4, predictions 7. 11, murders
8. 14, killed 9. 5, sleeps 10. 6, guards
11. 12, revenge 12. 7, victims
13. 10, visions 14. 2, witches

29–34 Answers will vary.

NAME _____   DATE _____

Read the Introduction at the front of *Macbeth*.

1. Macbeth is set in the year 1040. How long ago was that? _____

    If the average lifetime is 70 years, about how many
    lifetimes have gone by since then?   _____

2. What word or words in the Introduction suggest that this play is *not* a comedy?

    _____

3. After reading the Introduction, study the
    book's cover. Which character do you
    think is pictured in the *background*?   _____

4. Macbeth himself is pictured in the *foreground* of the cover. In what way does
    this picture show what you already know about Macbeth?

    _____

    _____

5. Have you ever known anyone who seemed *too* driven by ambition? What did
    that person say or do suggesting that ambition had taken over his or her life?

    _____

    _____

6. Suppose you had a friend who seemed ready to do something reckless in the
    name of ambition. What advice would you give him or her?

    _____

    _____

7. The world has changed a lot since 1040. Do you think people's motivations
    have changed, too? Explain your reasoning.

    _____

    _____

NAME _____   DATE _____

Circle a letter to answer each question.

1. When and where do the witches meet Macbeth for the first time?

   a. after the battle, before sunset, on the heath

   b. before the battle, after sunset, on the prairie

   c. during the battle, at sunrise, at Inverness

2. What is Macbeth's reward for bravery on the battlefield?

   a. He is made king.

   b. He is named Thane of Cawdor.

   c. King Duncan visits him at Inverness.

3. What do the witches tell Macbeth?

   a. that he will be the father of kings

   b. that he will be king

   c. that he will live a long and happy life

4. Why is the former Thane of Cawdor executed?

   a. for treason

   b. for cowardice

   c. for deserting his post

5. What does Lady Macbeth see as a great failing in Macbeth?

   a. that he is too cruel and ruthless

   b. that he is too kind and honest

   c. that he is too timid and shy

6. Who meets Duncan when he first gets to Inverness?

   a. Macbeth

   b. Banquo

   c. Lady Macbeth

7. What does Lady Macbeth talk her husband into doing?

   a. moving to England

   b. overthrowing King Duncan

   c. killing King Duncan

WORDS AND MEANINGS

NAME _____ DATE _____

A. Find and circle the hidden vocabulary words from Act 1. Words may go up, down, across, backward, or diagonally. Check off each word as you find it.

___ **FILTHY**	___ **EMBRACE**
___ **VILLAIN**	___ **STRENGTH**
___ **FANTASIES**	___ **CRUELTY**
___ **VANISHED**	___ **DAGGERS**
___ **PROPHECY**	___ **MURDER**
___ **PROSPER**	___ **THUNDER**

```
A K X P K Y H T L I F G
Z Q V A N I S H E D R E
Y P S T R E N G T H E D
G R M R H M P N J W P Y
L O U N I U A O V J S T
F P R S I T N C N I O L
E H D Q U A E D V H R E
Z E E B M H L W E U P U
C C R C A D Y L X R M R
L Y F A N T A S I E S C
F C S R E G G A D V B S
G D E M B R A C E T F B
```

B. Now complete each sentence with one or more of the hidden words.

1. The crime of deliberately taking someone's life is called

   _____.

2. If something is very dirty, it is _____.

3. Storms are often accompanied by _____ and lightning.

4. After the _____ committed his crime, he

   _____ and no one saw him again.

5. Things that are only imagined and not real are called

   _____.

6. The fortune teller's _____ was that the questioner

   would _____ in his business.

7. _____ to animals is a crime.

8. Another word for *knives* is _____.

9. The _____ of his _____ made

   me think of a bear hug.

 Saddleback Educational Publishing © 2003 • Three Watson, Irvine, CA 92618 • Phone: (888) 735-2225 • Fax: (888) 734-4010 • www.sdlback.com

CHARACTER STUDY

NAME _____   DATE _____

A. *Who's who?* First, unscramble the names of some of the characters you met in
Act 1. Then answer each question with one of the unscrambled names.

CATHMEB _____		**TWCIH** _____	
IDESLOR _____		**QUANBO** _____	
NIDKGCANUN _____		**SORS** _____	
DACHLYBAEMT _____			

1. Who reports that Macbeth and Banquo
   were brave in battle?   _____

2. Who tells Duncan of the Thane of
   Cawdor's treachery?   _____

3. Who fights next to Macbeth in battle?   _____

4. Who gives Macbeth a new title?   _____

5. Who vanishes like bubbles in the air?   _____

6. Who has the idea of killing Duncan?   _____

7. Who must be persuaded to kill Duncan?   _____

B. *Who said what?* Write a character's name next to the line that he or she spoke.

1. _____: "Look like the innocent flower / But be the serpent
   under it."

2. _____: "What he has lost, noble Macbeth has won."

3. _____: "A drum, a drum! / Macbeth does come."

4. _____: "So foul and fair a day I have not seen."

5. _____: "But I am faint. My wounds cry out!"

6. _____: "We forbade him to bury his men / Until he paid
   us $10,000."

7. _____: "New honors come upon Macbeth. / Like new
   clothes, they do not fit well / Until they've been
   used for a while."

SYNONYMS AND ANTONYMS

NAME _____   DATE _____

A. Complete the crossword puzzle with words from Act 1. The **boldface** clue words are *synonyms* (words with similar meanings) of the answer words.

ACROSS

2. was so **tired** / From running
3. Didn't this **worry** / Our captains
5. with his **previous** title
7. In the name of **honesty**

DOWN

1. has confessed to **treachery**
3. your brave **actions**
4. can **foretell** the future
5. Norwegian **banners** fill the sky
6. On the **moor**

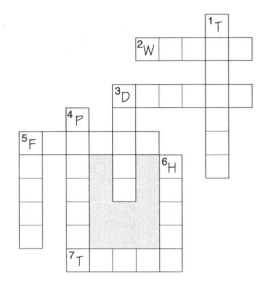

B. Read the phrases from Act 1. Then find the *antonym* (word that means the opposite) in the box for each **boldface** word. Write the antonym on the line.

weakness	failure	fresh	guilty	hello
ordinary	release	past	shallow	dull

1. fought against my **capture**

   _____

2. shake hands or say **farewell**

   _____

3. with greater **strength**

   _____

4. these creatures, so **withered**

   _____

5. this **strange** information

   _____

6. evidence of **success**

   _____

7. black and **deep** desires

   _____

8. my **keen** knife

   _____

9. like the **innocent** flower

   _____

10. hopes / For the **future**

   _____

RECALLING DETAILS

NAME _____   DATE _____

A. *Scenes 1 and 2:* Write **T** or **F** to show whether each statement is *true* or *false*.

1. _____ Three witches plan to meet Macbeth on a heath.

2. _____ A wounded soldier fought against the capture of King Duncan.

3. _____ Banquo and Macbeth fought bravely in a battle against Norway's forces.

4. _____ Norway's king refused to surrender.

5. _____ Duncan sentences the Thane of Cawdor to death for treason.

B. *Scenes 3 and 4:* Find the error or errors in each sentence. Then rewrite the sentences correctly on the writing lines.

1. Macbeth and Banquo meet four witches on a heath near Forres.

   _____

2. The witches tell Macbeth that his sons and grandsons will be king.

   _____

3. Banquo completely trusts what the witches have said.

   _____

4. Duncan appoints his youngest son Donalbain as his successor.

   _____

C. *Scenes 5–7:* Circle the word or phrase that correctly completes each sentence.

1. Macbeth tells his wife what the witches said (in a letter / in person).

2. Lady Macbeth decides that (Duncan must be killed / they should be patient).

3. Duncan thinks Macbeth's castle is (drafty and uncomfortable / located in a pleasant place).

4. Macbeth and Lady Macbeth plan to blame the murder on Duncan's (sons / guards).

NAME _____   DATE _____

Circle a letter to answer each question or complete a statement.

1. According to Banquo, when King Duncan decided to go to sleep, he was

   a. suspicious of Macbeth and Lady Macbeth.

   b. in a good mood and very content.

   c. wishing he could be at his own home instead.

2. The only reason Lady Macbeth doesn't kill King Duncan herself is that

   a. she is afraid of going to trial.

   b. he looks too much like her own father in his sleep.

   c. she is not ruthless enough.

3. What does Lady Macbeth say she will do to make the guards seem guilty?

   a. put daggers in their hands

   b. talk about them behind their backs

   c. smear their faces with blood

4. Why do Macduff and Lennox knock on the door of Macbeth's castle?

   a. They suspect that Macbeth has murdered King Duncan.

   b. They are hungry and want Macbeth to feed them.

   c. They had been told to call on the king at an early hour.

5. Who kills Duncan's guards?

   a. Macbeth

   b. Lady Macbeth

   c. Macduff

6. Why do Malcolm and Donalbain decide to leave Scotland?

   a. They are afraid they will be suspected of their father's murder.

   b. They fear that their father's murderer will also want to kill them.

   c. They have always wanted to travel to England and Ireland.

7. Who do Ross and Macduff think are responsible for Duncan's murder?

   a. Malcolm and Donalbain

   b. Macbeth and Lady Macbeth

   c. Banquo and Fleance

NAME _____   DATE _____

A. Find and circle the hidden vocabulary words from Act 2. Words may go up, down, across, backward, or diagonally. Check off each word as you find it.

R	L	A	Q	L	L	E	W	E	R	A	F
S	S	O	S	S	U	O	I	R	E	S	P
L	B	C	Y	A	U	R	D	Q	Z	C	O
U	T	A	U	A	V	F	P	D	F	R	R
M	T	R	E	G	L	R	R	D	C	E	E
B	A	R	F	X	O	I	V	O	W	A	B
E	W	I	Y	Y	E	G	K	N	J	M	M
R	Z	E	I	W	H	H	E	E	I	K	A
I	A	D	B	G	N	T	B	N	C	L	H
N	J	K	L	I	K	E	L	Y	O	L	C
G	C	J	E	L	H	N	I	M	D	D	E
S	E	C	R	E	T	N	X	M	F	D	G

___ **DONE**   ___**WEIRD**

___ **LOYAL**   ___ **SECRET**

___ **CHAMBER**   ___ **LIKELY**

___ **FAREWELL**   ___ **CARRIED**

___ **FRIGHTEN**   ___ **SERIOUS**

___ **SLUMBERING**   ___ **SCREAM**

B. Now complete each sentence with one or more of the hidden words.

1. If scary things _____ you, you may

   _____ very loudly.

2. Another word for *goodbye* is _____.

3. Difficult projects are not _____ to get

   _____ as quickly as easy ones.

4. If something is very strange, you might say it is _____.

5. A _____ friend will help you when you need help.

6. Dogs may keep watch outside your _____ when you

   are _____.

7. If you have a _____ problem, you might need someone
   to help you solve it.

8. The old man _____ a deep, dark _____
   to his grave.

NAME _____   DATE _____

A. *Who's who?* First, unscramble the names of some of the characters you met in Act 2. Then answer each question with one of the unscrambled names.

AOBQUN	_____	NXLOEN	_____
FAUMDCF	_____	LLMMCAO	_____
ATCHEMB	_____	SROS	_____
HTDCAAMBEYL	_____	NOLNDBIAA	_____

1. Who sees an imaginary dagger? _____

2. Who tells Macbeth that the king has gone to bed? _____

3. Who decides to go to England? _____

4. Who decides to go to Ireland? _____

5. Who pretends to faint upon hearing about Duncan's murder? _____

6. Which two people come to see Duncan in the morning? _____ and _____

7. Who goes to Scone to see Macbeth's coronation? _____

B. *Who said what?* Write the character's name next to the line that he or she spoke.

1. _____: "The sleeping and the dead are but pictures / Of each other."

2. _____: "Where we are now, there are daggers / In men's smiles."

3. _____: "Why would / They want to kill their own father?"

4. _____: "The owl shrieked all night."

5. _____: "The murderous arrow / That's been shot has not yet landed."

6. _____: "Confusion has made its masterpiece."

7. _____: "A heavy feeling lies on me like lead . . ."

8. _____: "The wine of life has been poured. / Only the dregs are left."

SYNONYMS AND ANTONYMS

NAME _____   DATE _____

A. Complete the crossword puzzle with words from Act 2. The **boldface** clue words are *synonyms* (words with similar meanings) of the answer words.

ACROSS

1. are you, **deadly** vision
3. **scorn** their king with snores
4. He was in a good **humor**.
6. safer if we are **apart**
7. **evil** dreams come

DOWN

1. such **ridiculous** thoughts
2. or we will go **insane**
4. But what was their **reason**?
5. there was **crying** heard

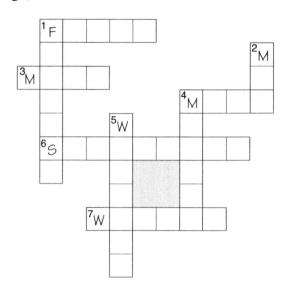

B. Read the phrases from Act 2. Then find the *antonym* (word that means the opposite) in the box for each **boldface** word. Write the antonym on the line.

arriving	artificial	dirty	first	good
wastefulness	restores	waking	rough	kind

1. There is **thriftiness** in the heavens.

   _____

2. I can see you still, in a form as **real**

   _____

3. says the **last** good night

   _____

4. and not the deed, **ruins** us

   _____

5. go to our chamber and **wash** our hands

   _____

6. as if we've been **sleeping**

   _____

7. Is the king **leaving** today?

   _____

8. Shake off this **gentle** sleep.

   _____

9. It would be too **cruel** anywhere.

   _____

10. forces of / Treason and **evil**

   _____

ANALYZING SIMILES AND METAPHORS

NAME _____   DATE _____

A *simile* compares two unlike things, using *like* or *as*.

  EXAMPLE: Her smile was *like a sunbeam*.

A *metaphor* compares two unlike things, without using *like* or *as*.

  EXAMPLE: The moon *was a golden balloon*.

Write *simile* or *metaphor* to identify each figure of speech below. Then write another example expressing the same idea. The first one has been done as an example.

1. There is thriftiness in the heavens, / For **the stars, like candles, are all out**.

   This is an example of a _____*simile*_____.

   MY EXAMPLE: *the stars, like lamps, have been turned off*

2. A heavy feeling **lies on me like lead**.

   This is an example of a _____.

   MY EXAMPLE: _____

3. **sleep that / Knits up the raveled sleeve of care**

   This is an example of a _____.

   MY EXAMPLE: _____

4. **sleep . . . / The death of each day's worries**

   This is an example of a _____.

   MY EXAMPLE: _____

5. The sleeping and the dead **are but pictures / Of each other**

   This is an example of a _____.

   MY EXAMPLE: _____

6. The **wine of life has been poured**. / Only the dregs are left.

   This is an example of a _____.

   MY EXAMPLE: _____

 Saddleback Educational Publishing © 2003 • Three Watson, Irvine, CA 92618 • Phone: (888) 735-2225 • Fax: (888) 734-4010 • www.sdlback.com

COMPREHENSION CHECK

Circle a letter to answer each question.

1. Why does Macbeth want to have Banquo and Fleance killed?

   a. He is afraid they will find out that he killed Duncan.

   b. He doesn't want the witches' prophecies to come true.

   c. He knows that they are jealous of him.

2. How does Macbeth get the two murderers to agree to kill Banquo and Fleance?

   a. He pays them a lot of money.

   b. He promises them important positions in his court.

   c. He says that Banquo had wronged them in the past.

3. Before the banquet, what advice does Macbeth give Lady Macbeth about how to behave?

   a. to show honor to Banquo both with her eyes and with her words

   b. to be very quiet during the banquet so other people could talk freely

   c. to act grief-stricken about Duncan's death

4. In what way do the murderers fail in their mission for Macbeth?

   a. They kill Fleance but not Banquo.

   b. They kill Banquo but not Fleance.

   c. Both Banquo and Fleance get away.

5. What causes Macbeth's strange behavior at the banquet?

   a. He has a bad headache.

   b. The food gives him indigestion.

   c. He sees Banquo's ghost.

6. After Macbeth says the ghost is gone, what does Lady Macbeth ask the guests to do?

   a. leave immediately

   b. stay for dessert

   c. come back tomorrow for another feast

7. How does Lennox feel about Macbeth?

   a. Macbeth is a worthy king who deserves support.

   b. Macbeth is a murderer who must be overthrown.

   c. Macbeth is an ineffective but well-meaning ruler.

NAME _____ DATE _____

A. Find and circle the hidden vocabulary words from Act 3. Words may go up, down, across, backward, or diagonally. Check off each word as you find it.

U	E	G	J	G	R	A	C	I	O	U	S
V	F	B	T	Q	Y	Z	M	E	A	P	A
G	O	S	S	F	W	S	T	B	U	O	D
N	R	D	K	S	X	M	N	B	I	O	B
I	T	O	J	T	T	N	E	M	L	I	A
S	U	H	K	S	W	H	D	U	H	N	C
S	N	T	L	E	M	H	I	V	D	C	H
E	E	E	G	U	N	E	C	E	R	T	S
L	P	M	O	G	Q	A	C	R	U	F	K
B	L	A	C	Y	M	L	A	O	H	T	S
B	A	N	Q	U	E	T	Y	R	I	G	A
J	M	Q	I	D	F	H	X	Z	S	D	M

___ GUESTS   ___ DOUBTS

___ MASKS   ___ ACCIDENT

___ FORTUNE   ___ YOUTH

___ HEALTH   ___ AILMENT

___ GRACIOUS   ___ METHODS

___ BANQUET   ___ BLESSING

B. Now complete each sentence with one or more of the hidden words.

1. The best _____ anyone can have may be good _____ .

2. People can disguise their faces with _____ .

3. Fourteen _____ were at the _____ , enjoying the elaborate meal.

4. I have no _____ about your honesty.

5. The _____ host made the guests feel welcome.

6. In her _____ , the old woman had been crippled in a car _____ .

7. The financial expert shared his _____ of creating a _____ .

8. The doctors could not find the cause of his _____ .

NAME _____   DATE _____

A. *Who did it?* Write the name of the character who took each action described below. Choose from the characters listed in the box. Check off each name as you use it.

> ___ **Murderer 1**   ___ **Macbeth**   ___ **Murderer 2**   ___ **Lord**
> ___ **Lady Macbeth**   ___ **Lennox**   ___ **Banquo**

1. Who talks with Lennox about what Malcolm and Macduff are doing?   _____

2. Who goes out riding the day of the banquet?   _____

3. Who talks with Macbeth about killing Banquo?   _____ and _____

4. Who sees a ghost at the banquet?   _____

5. Who suspects that Macbeth killed the guards to keep them from denying their guilt?   _____

6. Who asks the banquet guests to leave?   _____

B. *Who said what?* Write a character's name next to the line that he or she spoke.

1. _____: "Run, run, run! Avenge me later! Farewell!"

2. _____: "We may again live in peace someday, / Without fear of bloody knives at banquets."

3. _____: "Nothing is ours, all is spent, / When we have our desire but are not content."

4. _____: "Be innocent of the knowledge / Until you applaud the deed."

5. _____: "May a swift blessing soon return / To our suffering country!"

6. _____: "I am reckless about what I do / To spite the world."

7. _____: "I would bet my life on any chance / To mend it or be rid of it."

NAME _____   DATE _____

A. Complete the crossword puzzle with words from Act 3. The **boldface** clue words are *synonyms* (words with similar meanings) of the answer words.

ACROSS

2. our suffering **nation**
4. battle as my **hero**
6. I am **foolhardy**.
8. Your **desire** is my command.
9. at the **correct** time

DOWN

1. A **terrible** deed shall be done.
3. Questions **anger** him.
5. begins to droop and **sleep**
7. take any **form**

B. Read the phrases from Act 3. Then find the *antonym* (word that means the opposite) in the box for each **boldface** word. Write the antonym on the line.

admit	better	guilty	sickness	honor
lively	proud	expose	sorrowful	weak

1. If so, I have **strong** hopes.

_____

2. my **innocent** self

_____

3. so **weary** / With disasters

_____

4. That's comforting, so be **joyful**.

_____

5. and play the **humble** host

_____

6. Now, good **health** to all!

_____

7. make it **worse**

_____

8. Let the earth **hide** you!

_____

9. hear the guards **deny** it

_____

10. Macduff lives in **disgrace**, too.

_____

FINDING CAUSE AND EFFECT

NAME _____   DATE _____

The chart below lists several events that occur in Act 3. In some places, the *cause* of the action or event has been given. In other places, the *effect* is listed. Fill in the blank spaces. The first one has been completed as an example.

CAUSE	EFFECT
1. *Macbeth is afraid that he will lose the crown to one of Banquo's sons.*	Macbeth gets murderers to kill Banquo and his son, Fleance.
Macbeth lies to the murderers, saying it was Banquo who had betrayed them and brought ruin to them.	2.
One of the murderers strikes out the light Fleance had been carrying.	3.
4.	Macbeth leaves his guests for a minute to talk to the murderer.
5.	Lady Macbeth calls Macbeth back to the table to give the toast.
The ghost of Banquo appears and sits in Macbeth's place at the table.	6.
7.	Lady Macbeth tells the guests to eat and pay no attention to Macbeth.
8.	Lady Macbeth asks the guests to leave.
Macduff does not come to the banquet, nor does he send a messenger with an excuse.	9.
Lennox suggests that Macbeth is responsible for the deaths of Duncan, the two guards, and Banquo.	10.

NAME _____   DATE _____

Circle a letter to answer each question.

1. Where does Macbeth find the three witches?

   a. in a dark cave

   b. on the heath

   c. at Inverness

2. What do the witches show Macbeth?

   a. Banquo's ghost sitting at a banquet table

   b. where Fleance is hiding

   c. three visions suggesting events in the future

3. Why is Lady Macduff angry with her husband?

   a. because he didn't invite her to the banquet at Inverness

   b. because he took a vacation without her

   c. because he left Scotland, leaving her unprotected

4. What happens to Lady Macduff?

   a. She dies of a serious illness.

   b. She is murdered by men sent by Macbeth.

   c. She becomes a servant in Macbeth's castle.

5. Why does Malcolm tell Macduff that he, Malcolm, has many great failings?

   a. He is testing Macduff to see how much he loves Scotland.

   b. He wants Macduff to know the truth about him.

   c. He wants to make Macduff afraid of him.

6. What terrible news does Ross bring to Macduff?

   a. that his wife is very ill

   b. that one of his children has died

   c. that his wife, children, and servants have been killed

7. Who will help Malcolm and Macduff overthrow Macbeth?

   a. the King of England

   b. the King of Norway

   c. the King of France

WORDS AND MEANINGS

NAME _____   DATE _____

A. Find and circle the hidden vocabulary words from Act 4. Words may go up, down, across, backward, or diagonally. Check off each word as you find it.

___ **VIRTUOUS**	___ **SUFFER**
___ **POWERFUL**	___ **WEEP**
___ **COMMAND**	___ **SWAMP**
___ **NATURAL**	___ **FOREST**
___ **QUARRELS**	___ **STINGY**
___ **TRUSTWORTHY**	___ **RUMOR**

```
T  R  U  S  T  W  O  R  T  H  Y  A
C  F  Y  H  X  E  Q  R  U  N  C  G
N  O  G  K  P  A  E  T  V  A  O  S
Y  R  N  Z  W  F  B  I  E  T  M  F
K  E  I  V  F  S  R  L  C  U  M  G
F  S  T  U  J  T  U  L  D  R  A  L
M  T  S  I  U  F  P  I  T  A  N  U
L  G  O  O  R  Q  E  R  R  L  D  H
L  H  U  E  P  D  E  W  O  J  B  V
M  S  W  K  N  E  W  F  M  C  Y  Z
I  O  S  W  A  M  P  X  U  M  A  B
P  D  O  J  Q  U  A  R  R  E  L  S
```

B. Now complete each sentence with one or more of the hidden words.

1. If you try to be good and avoid evil, you will probably be seen as _____.

2. When a loved one is hurt, it is a _____ reaction to _____.

3. _____ between family members can destroy peace in a home.

4. Our friendship will _____ if you show that you are not _____.

5. This dog refuses to obey any _____.

6. Would you rather live near a _____ or a _____?

7. A _____ is a story that usually travels very fast.

8. That rich and _____ man is far too _____ with his money.

NAME _____   DATE _____

A. *Who did it?* Write the name of the character who took each action described below. Choose from the characters listed in the box. Check off each name as you use it.

___ Witches	___ Vision 2	___ Macbeth	___ Ross
___ Lady Macduff	___ Malcolm	___ Macduff	

1. Who brings the news to Macduff about what happened to his wife and children?   _____

2. Who wants to take back his rightful crown from Macbeth?   _____

3. Who appears to Macbeth from out of the witches' cauldron?   _____

4. Which characters show a series of visions to Macbeth?   _____

5. Who tells her son that his father is a traitor?   _____

6. Who punishes Macduff by having his family killed?   _____

7. Who joins forces with Malcolm against Macbeth?   _____

B. *Who said what?* Write a character's name next to the line that he or she spoke.

1. _____: "Macbeth is like fruit ripe on the tree, / Ready for shaking."

2. _____: "Double, double, toil and trouble. / Fire, burn, and cauldron, bubble."

3. _____: "All my pretty ones? Did you say all? *All?*"

4. _____: "Good men's lives end / Before the flowers in their caps wither."

5. _____: "Even the wren, the smallest of birds, / Will fight the owl to protect her babies."

6. _____: "I will not boast about it like a fool. / This deed I'll do before my anger cools."

7. _____: "Laugh to scorn the power of man, for / None of woman born shall harm Macbeth!"

SYNONYMS AND ANTONYMS

NAME _____   DATE _____

A. Complete the crossword puzzle with words from Act 4. The **boldface** clue words are *synonyms* (words with similar meanings) of the answer words.

ACROSS

1. I know my **shortcomings**.
4. Round about the **pot** go.
6. Was my father a **betrayer**?
7. yet my heart **beats**
9. his **consent** to leave

DOWN

2. to **satisfy** an angry god
3. Do not worry about your **foes**.
5. I am also **selfish**.
8. who mean to do you **wrong**

B. Read the phrases from Act 4. Then find the *antonym* (word that means the opposite) in the box for each **boldface** word. Write the antonym on the line.

weak	doubtful	deceptive	gentle	public
noisy	poverty	fortunate	virtues	appear

1. a charm of **powerful** trouble

   _____

2. just to be **sure**

   _____

3. The witches dance and then **vanish**.

   _____

4. all **unlucky** relatives

   _____

5. Why, the **honest** men.

   _____

6. I grant that he is **brutal**.

   _____

7. destroying them for **wealth**

   _____

8. But why are you **silent**?

   _____

9. Or is it a **private** grief?

   _____

10. not for their **faults**, but for mine

   _____

NAME _____   DATE _____

Read each sentence and think about the words in **boldface** type. Then complete each *analogy* (comparison of likeness) by choosing the best word and writing it on the line.

1. "Double, double, **toil** and trouble."

   ANALOGY: *Truthful* is to *honest* as *toil* is to _____.

   dishonest   play   work   trouble

2. "Tell me if Banquo's sons / Shall ever **reign** in this kingdom."

   ANALOGY: *Sight* is to *site* as *reign* is to _____.

   rule   king   rain   reigning

3. "We float upon a **wild** and violent sea, / Moving each way the waves take us."

   ANALOGY: *Warm* is to *cool* as _____ is to *wild*.

   calm   ferocious   wilder   untamed

4. "That makes me / Think that you might still be **loyal** to him."

   ANALOGY: *Priority* is to *prior* as _____ is to *loyal*.

   brave   loyalty   disloyal   royal

5. "But I **beg** your pardon for these thoughts."

   ANALOGY: *Declare* is to *state* as *beg* is to _____.

   demand   beggar   declaration   ask

6. "The state will regard him as a **lamb**, / compared to my endless harms."

   ANALOGY: *Lamb* is to _____ as *chicken* is to *feathers*.

   wool   meat   ewe   sheep

NAME _____   DATE _____

Circle a letter to answer each question.

1. What is Lady Macbeth doing as the doctor and the woman are watching her?

   a. resting

   b. sleepwalking

   c. writing letters

2. Where will Angus and his forces meet the English army to march against Macbeth?

   a. near Birnam Wood

   b. at the Scottish border

   c. in the witches' cave

3. Why is Macbeth not afraid of Malcolm?

   a. because he knows Malcolm has little battle experience

   b. because he knows that Malcolm is afraid of him

   c. because Malcolm was born of a woman

4. What does Malcolm tell his soldiers to hide behind?

   a. branches cut down from the trees of Birnam Wood

   b. their shields and armor

   c. any tree, rock, or natural feature in the land

5. What bad news about Lady Macbeth does Seyton bring to Macbeth?

   a. that she is insane

   b. that she has a serious disease

   c. that she is dead

6. Why does Macbeth want to avoid fighting Macduff?

   a. because he has already harmed Macduff too greatly

   b. because he is afraid of Macduff

   c. because he thinks too highly of Macduff

7. How does Macbeth finally realize the meaning of the prophecy that "none of woman born" could harm him?

   a. He goes to the witches and demands a clearer explanation.

   b. Just before Macduff kills Macbeth, he tells him that his birth was not normal.

   c. He finally decides to kill himself rather than be killed in battle.

NAME _____   DATE _____

A. Find and circle the hidden vocabulary words from Act 5. Words may go up, down, across, backward, or diagonally. Check off each word as you find it.

___ **WITNESS**   ___ **FURY**

___ **CHALLENGE**   ___ **STRUTS**

___ **PERFUMES**   ___ **TYRANT**

___ **MOURNING**   ___ **WORTH**

___ **MEDICINE**   ___ **EXILED**

___ **HEALTHY**   ___ **INVITE**

```
E G C D E L I X E B P A
H M E D I C I N E K E P
S D S R F V Q S W O R L
T I E U M J S W O X F Y
R T W G I E F U R Y U H
U N X L N V U O T M M T
T Y Z T V E K B H Y E L
S O I C I T L A N Z S A
P W D Q T R I L J A B E
E K H R E T Y R A N T H
M O U R N I N G G H F C
L P I S F J G H X E C D
```

B. Now complete each sentence with one or more of the hidden words.

1. A _____ to a crime is someone who saw it happen.

2. A _____ is someone who rules without considering the benefit of the people he rules.

3. If you get sick, _____ might help you get _____ again.

4. After a loved one dies, the survivors go through a period of _____.

5. The proud man _____ around, showing off like a peacock.

6. By having a tantrum, the child expressed his _____ at being denied a new toy.

7. Fancy French _____ are _____ a lot of money.

8. It is sometimes a difficult _____ to _____ only compatible people to a party.

9. If a person is forced to leave his own country, he is _____.

CHARACTER STUDY

NAME _____ DATE _____

A. *Who did it?* Write the name of the character who took each action described below. Choose from the characters listed in the box. Check off each name as you use it.

___ **Gentlewoman**	___ **Doctor**	___ **Macbeth**	___ **Ross**
___ **Lady Macbeth**	___ **Malcolm**	___ **Seyton**	

1. Who tells Macbeth that he cannot help Lady Macbeth? _____

2. Who tells Siward that his son has been killed? _____

3. Who becomes king after Macbeth is killed? _____

4. Whose sleep is disturbed by feelings of guilt? _____

5. Who thinks he cannot be killed by any man? _____

6. Who watches with the doctor while Lady Macbeth sleepwalks? _____

7. Who tells Macbeth that his wife is dead? _____

B. *Who said what?* Write a character's name next to the line that he or she spoke.

1. _____: "She rises from bed, takes out a paper, folds it, writes on it, and reads it."

2. _____: "All the perfumes of Arabia will not sweeten this little hand."

3. _____: "The queen, my lord, is dead."

4. _____: "Tomorrow, and tomorrow, and tomorrow, / Creeps on this petty pace from day to day . . ."

5. _____: "He lived only until he was a man, / Then like a man he died."

6. _____: "We shall soon call our exiled friends home, / And bring to trial the cruel ministers / Of this dead butcher and his fiendish queen . . ."

7. _____: "In cases like this, the patient / Must minister to himself."

NAME _____ DATE _____

A. Complete the crossword puzzle with words from Act 5. The **boldface** clue words are *synonyms* (words with similar meanings) of the answer words.

ACROSS

1. by her **order**, she always
4. which will not **surrender**
6. She needs **heavenly** help.
7. our castle's **sturdiness**
8. **miserable** soldiers, who fight

DOWN

1. **heal** her of that
2. this **illness** is beyond
3. troubled with **sights**
5. be **ridiculed** by the commoners

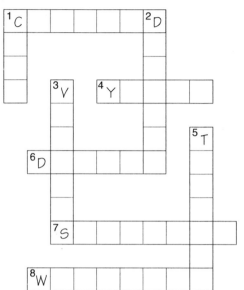

B. Read the phrases from Act 5. Then find the *antonym* (word that means the opposite) in the box for each **boldface** word. Write the antonym on the line.

genius	defeat	destroying	forgiveness	friends
cowardly	never	important	remembered	quietly

1. She **always** has light by her bedside.
   _____

2. Desire for **revenge** burns in them.
   _____

3. **protecting** his castle
   _____

4. I have almost **forgotten**
   _____

5. creeps on this **petty** pace
   _____

6. a tale / Told by an **idiot**
   _____

7. **brave** Macduff and I
   _____

8. **loudly** sing of blood and death
   _____

9. **Victory** soon declares itself yours.
   _____

10. We have met with some **foes**.
   _____

CONSIDERING POINT OF VIEW

NAME _____   DATE _____

The following sentences do not appear in Act 5—but suppose they did.
Who might have said each one? Write the name of the character on the line.
Use each of these names twice:

Macbeth   Lady Macbeth   Doctor   Gentlewoman   Malcolm   Macduff

1. "I'll get back at the tyrant for killing my
   father and creating such turmoil."   _____

2. "I put a candle by her bed every night,
   as she has requested."   _____

3. "I never should have talked my husband
   into murdering Duncan."   _____

4. "I never should have trusted what those
   witches revealed to me."   _____

5. "I haven't been able to reach my brother
   Donalbain to ask for his help in this battle."   _____

6. "I won't tell the doctor what she said
   because he'd never believe me."   _____

7. "Perhaps one of my colleagues might be
   able to help Lady Macbeth."   _____

8. "What a monster he is to have ordered the
   deaths of my wife and children!"   _____

9. "The only way I can end my mental
   suffering is to take my own life."   _____

10. "The only one I want to kill in this
    battle is Macbeth himself, for what he
    did to my family."   _____

11. "In all my years of practice, I have
    never seen a case like this."   _____

12. "I guess it's fitting that Macduff should
    be the one to kill me, after all the harm
    I inflicted on his family."   _____

NAME _____   DATE _____

A. Write two sentences about each of the following characters. In the first sentence, describe a quality in that character's personality. In the second sentence, tell something the character does that demonstrates that quality.

1. **Macbeth:** _____

_____

_____

2. **Lady Macbeth:** _____

_____

_____

3. **Banquo:** _____

_____

_____

4. **Duncan:** _____

_____

_____

5. **Malcolm:** _____

_____

_____

6. **Macduff:** _____

_____

_____

B. For each character, find a quotation from the play that indicates the quality you described in Part A.

1. **Macbeth:** _____

_____

2. **Lady Macbeth:** _____

_____

3. **Banquo:** _____

_____

4. **Duncan:** _____

_____

5. **Malcolm:** _____

_____

6. **Macduff:** _____

_____

NAME _____ DATE _____

Circle a letter to correctly answer each question or complete each statement.

1. Most events in this play takes place in

    a. England.

    b. Denmark.

    c. Scotland.

    d. Italy.

2. Where were Macbeth and Banquo coming *from* when they first met the witches?

    a. a battlefield in Scotland

    b. King Duncan's castle at Dunsinane

    c. Macbeth's castle at Inverness

    d. Birnam Wood

3. How did Lady Macbeth learn about what the witches had told Macbeth?

    a. Banquo told her.

    b. The witches appeared to her later.

    c. Macbeth spoke to her about it.

    d. Macbeth wrote about it in a letter.

4. At first, who gets blamed for King Duncan's murder?

    a. guards hired by Duncan's sons

    b. Fleance

    c. the three witches

    d. Banquo

5. What frightens Macbeth at the banquet?

    a. the ghost of King Duncan

    b. the vision of Banquo's ghost

    c. the vision of a crowned child

    d. a visit from the murderers

6. Why does Malcolm tell his soldiers to hold branches in front of them?

    a. to hide completely

    b. for greater protection in battle

    c. to fulfill a prophecy

    d. so that Macbeth's spies can't count them

NAME _____   DATE _____

Answer each question in your own words. Write in complete sentences.

1. Why does Macbeth kill the guards who had been sleeping outside Duncan's door?

   _____

   _____

   _____

2. Why does Lady Macbeth have trouble sleeping at night?

   _____

   _____

   _____

3. Why does Macbeth want Banquo and Fleance to be killed?

   _____

   _____

   _____

4. Why does Macduff go to England, leaving his wife and children alone and unprotected?

   _____

   _____

   _____

5. Why does Lady Macbeth commit suicide?

   _____

   _____

   _____

6. Explain what was so misleading about the prophecies revealed by the witches.

   _____

   _____

   _____

NAME _____   DATE _____

First, complete the sentences with words from the box. Then, number the events to show which happened first, second, and so on.

banquet	courage	escapes	guards	killed	walks	murders
predictions	revenge	visions	victims	sleeps	visits	witches

_____ 1. At Macbeth's urging, murderers kill Banquo, but Fleance
_____.

_____ 2. Banquo's ghost appears to Macbeth at a _____.

_____ 3. King Duncan _____ Macbeth and Lady Macbeth
at Inverness.

_____ 4. King Duncan gives the title "Thane of Cawdor" to Macbeth for
_____ on the battlefield.

_____ 5. Lady Macbeth _____ in her sleep, trying to wash
the blood off her hands.

_____ 6. Lady Macbeth reads a letter from Macbeth in which he tells about the
witches' _____.

_____ 7. Macbeth gives the order for the _____ of Macduff's
family, including his wife, children, and servants.

_____ 8. Macbeth is _____ by Macduff, and Malcolm
becomes King of Scotland.

_____ 9. Macbeth murders King Duncan as he _____.

_____ 10. Later, Macbeth kills the _____ who were sleeping
outside Duncan's room.

_____ 11. Malcolm urges Macduff to turn his grief into rage and get
_____ against Macbeth for his crimes.

_____ 12. Realizing that they could be the next _____,
Malcolm and Donalbain leave Scotland.

_____ 13. The witches reveal a series of _____ to Macbeth,
suggesting no one can kill him.

_____ 14. Three _____ tell Macbeth that he will be king.

Choose one "extra credit" project from each column. Complete the short-term project on the back of this sheet. To complete the second project, follow your teacher's instructions.

SHORT-TERM PROJECTS

1. Write brief captions for any of the four illustrations in the book.

2. Draw a picture of your favorite character. Be sure the clothing and hairstyles are appropriate to the times.

3. Write a diary entry for one of the main characters. Describe, from that character's point of view, one of the important events in the play.

4. Write appropriate titles for the first two or three scenes in Act 1.

5. Draw a simple map, showing various locations mentioned in the play.

6. Choose any page from the play, and rewrite all the dialogue.

7. Playing the role of a newspaper reporter, write a brief article describing one scene in the play.

LONG-TERM PROJECTS

1. Do some research to find out why Shakespeare was called an "upstart crow" by a rival playwright. Explain your findings.

2. Describe the system of government at the time this play was written. Use library resources to find the information.

3. Make a diorama depicting one of the important scenes in the play.

4. You be the playwright! In three or four paragraphs, explain your idea for a different ending of this play.

5. Make a "then and now" chart showing differences between Shakespeare's time and our time. Compare clothing, customs, and travel.

6. Read into a cassette recorder to make an audiotape of any two scenes from the play.

SHAKESPEARE PLAYS
THEME ANALYSIS: _____
(TITLE OF PLAY)

NAME _____   DATE _____

Review the Glossary definition of *theme*. Then study the literary themes listed in the box.

bravery	loyalty	revenge	revolution	nature	hope
guilt	love	friendship	repentance	courage	war
madness	science	injustice	greed	regret	youth

Authors often want to deliver a message about their themes. This message, usually a deeply held belief, is expressed in the story or play.

Think about the play you just read. What theme or themes can you recognize? What was the main idea? What point was the author trying to make about that theme? What message was delivered?

Choose two or three themes from the box, or write your own. Then write a sentence explaining the author's belief about that theme. (This kind of sentence is called a *thematic statement*.)

EXAMPLE: *The Crucible*, by Arthur Miller

   Theme: injustice

   Thematic statement: Hasty judgment because of prejudice
      can have tragic consequences for innocent individuals.

THEME 1: _____

THEMATIC STATEMENT: _____

_____

_____

THEME 2: _____

THEMATIC STATEMENT: _____

_____

_____

THEME 3: _____

THEMATIC STATEMENT: _____

_____

_____

CHARACTER STUDY: _____

NAME _____   DATE _____

Review the Glossary definition of *character*. Then name two important
characters from the play you just read. Write a brief description of each.

1. **CHARACTER:** _____

   DESCRIPTION: _____

   _____

2. **CHARACTER:** _____

   DESCRIPTION: _____

   _____

3. Which character did you find most interesting? _____

   Explain why. _____

   _____

4. Describe the main conflict this character faces.

   _____

   _____

5. How is this conflict finally resolved?

   _____

   _____

6. Does the plot's outcome make the character happy or unhappy? _____

   Explain how. _____

   _____

7. What information in the play helped you understand this character? Write three
   lines of dialogue or description.

   _____

   _____

   _____

8. On the back of this sheet, write a sentence telling how you and the character
   are **alike**. Then write another sentence telling how the two of you are **different**.

SHAKESPEARE PLAYS
VOCABULARY STUDY: _____
(TITLE OF PLAY)

NAME _____   DATE _____

Look back through the play you just read. Find 10 words that were new to you.
First, list the words on the lines below. Then check a dictionary if you're not sure
what each word means. Finally, use each word in a sentence of your own.

1. _____   6. _____

2. _____   7. _____

3. _____   8. _____

4. _____   9. _____

5. _____   10. _____

1. _____
   _____

2. _____
   _____

3. _____
   _____

4. _____
   _____

5. _____
   _____

6. _____
   _____

7. _____
   _____

8. _____
   _____

9. _____
   _____

10. _____
    _____

GLOSSARY STUDY: _____
(TITLE OF PLAY)

NAME _____   DATE _____

1. Review the Glossary definition of **conflict**. Then describe one example of a conflict in this play.

   _____

   _____

2. Review the Glossary definition of **figurative language**. Then find two examples in the play and write them on the lines.

   _____

   _____

3. Select your favorite short lines of **dialogue** from the play. Write them on the lines.

   _____

   _____

   _____

4. Describe the **setting** of the play. When and where does the story take place?

   _____

   _____

5. Review the Glossary definition of **motive**. Explain the motive, or driving force, behind the main character's actions.

   _____

   _____

6. Review the Glossary definition of **climax**. Then describe the outcome of the play's main conflict.

   _____

   _____

7. Think about a major event in the play. What was the main character's **point of view** about that event? Explain how the playwright revealed that character's point of view.

   _____

   _____

   _____

SHAKESPEARE PLAYS
CRITICAL REVIEW, PART 1: _____
(TITLE OF PLAY)

NAME _____   DATE _____

Imagine you are a theater critic for a newspaper. Your job is to tell your readers about the play you just saw. Before you write your review—which will contain both fact and opinion—you must take notes. Use this form to gather the information you will use in your article.

PLAY TITLE AND AUTHOR: _____

1. Imagine that you attended the gala opening-night performance. Name a fictional theater, and describe how the audience reacted to the play.

   _____

   _____

2. What *type* of play is this? (Examples: comedy, tragedy, mystery, action, etc.) Name more than one type, if appropriate.

   _____

3. Describe the *main character* in two or three sentences. Use meaningful details.

   _____

   _____

   _____

   _____

4. Describe two or three *supporting characters*. Explain each character's relationship to the main character.

   _____

   _____

   _____

   _____

   _____

5. Write one or two lines from the play as examples of powerful *description*. (Hint: Look for vivid sights, sounds, smells, or feelings.)

   _____

   _____

   _____

6. Write one or two lines from the play as examples of *figurative language*.

_____

_____

_____

7. Summarize the *plot* of the play in one brief paragraph. (Hint: Name one key event from the play's beginning, middle, and end.)

_____

_____

_____

_____

_____

_____

8. Choose one scene from the play and describe how the stage was decorated to suggest that place.

_____

_____

_____

9. Describe the actors' performances in two of the main roles. (Name two popular actors you think would have played the parts well.)

_____

_____

_____

_____

10. State two reasons why you **would** or **would not** recommend that your readers should attend this play.

_____

_____

_____

_____